The Powder Monkey

MAUREEN RYLANCE

Illustrated by Robin Lawrie

OXFORD
UNIVERSITY PRESS

OXFORD
UNIVERSITY PRESS

Great Clarendon Street, Oxford OX2 6DP

Oxford University Press is a department of the University of Oxford.
It furthers the University's objective of excellence in research, scholarship,
and education by publishing worldwide in

Oxford   New York

Auckland Bangkok Buenos Aires Cape Town Chennai
Dar es Salaam Delhi Hong Kong Istanbul Karachi Kolkata
Kuala Lumpur Madrid Melbourne Mexico City Mumbai Nairobi
São Paulo Shanghai Taipei Tokyo Toronto

Oxford is a registered trade mark of Oxford University Press
in the UK and in certain other countries

ISBN 0 19 918727 4

Printed in Great Britain

Illustrations by Robin Lawrie

Photograph of Maureen Rylance by David Walker

For Jessica

1

Getting ready to sail

Harry looked at the rat. It was on the shelf in front of him. Its beady eyes stared and its long whiskers twitched. He banged on the shelf with his fist, and the rat vanished behind some sacks.

Harry loved the store-room in the ship's chandler's. It was dusty and gloomy and the air was heavy with all sorts of smells, but to Harry, it was a really interesting place. He could put up with a few rats and cockroaches. When he went to sea in a couple of years, he would see plenty of those.

He looked around the store-room. Every bit of space was crammed with bundles, sacks, barrels and containers. Whatever captains wanted for their ships, they could get it here. Everyone said that Shadrach Pinchbeck had the finest chandler's store in the county. When Harry was captain of his own ship, he would buy his stores here.

In two more years he would be thirteen. Then no one could stop him from joining the King's Navy. He could hardly wait.

Harry suddenly realized that Shadrach was calling to him.

'Come on, lad, what are you doing? There's work to be done.'

Harry sighed and dragged a roll of sail canvas down from a shelf. He staggered into the shop and set it down on the floor. When Shadrach wasn't looking, he took a quick look out at the harbour.

People bustled about, fetching and carrying. The stallkeepers were doing a fine trade. There was a buzz of excitement in the air.

His Majesty's ship, the *Prosperity*, was getting ready to set sail. Its crew were going into battle to fight the French: to defend the country.

'Now, lad, I won't put up with daydreamers,' Shadrach said. 'Do you want to earn tuppence today or not?'

'Oh, yes, sir, I'm sorry,' said Harry. He knew how pleased his ma would be when he brought home two precious pennies.

'Right, well I'll read out the rest of the things from the list, and you get into the back and bring them out.'

Shadrach moved around carefully, dodging the hundreds of jugs, pots and canisters that hung from every part of the ceiling.

'And fast, mind you, or I'll let some other little scallywag have your job.'

'This is a lot of stuff for one ship,' Harry said, looking at the pile of stores on the floor.

'Well, a fine ship like the *Prosperity* needs plenty of stores to keep officers and crew going. Who knows how long they'll be away?

And this is only part of it. They'll have got stuff from the Navy yard as well.' Shadrach licked his pencil, and made marks on his list.

'Right, what's next? Ah, yes, eight lanterns and two boxes of sailmaker's needles.'

Harry scurried off into the musty store-room once more. When he returned, Shadrach was talking to a large, rough-looking man. His Navy jacket had several brass buttons missing, and he had a dirty black scarf knotted round his neck. In his hand, he held a short length of twisted rope.

Suddenly, he brought the rope down hard on to some sacks. Clouds of dust rose in the air. Harry jumped and stumbled back into the doorway of the store-room.

'Aye, that's a fine enough cat-o'-nine-tails. I usually make my own, but time's pressing. I'll have three more. I'll likely need them on this trip. There's always cowards who'll run away from hard work or a battle.'

He grinned, showing a mouth full of brown and black teeth.

'The captain wants to know how much longer you'll be. He wants to set sail on tonight's tide.'

'Everything will be ready in two hours,' Shadrach said.

After he had gone, Shadrach stood with his hands on his hips. He shook his head. 'There goes a cruel man, Harry,' he said.

'But who is he, sir?' Harry asked.

'That's the ship's bosun, from the *Prosperity*. God help the poor men working under him.'

'Was that rope thing used for hitting men?'

'Aye, the cat-o'-nine-tails has been used to discipline many a man. But there's some bad 'uns who enjoy using the tail on good men too.' He shook his head again.

Harry stared at him.

'In the King's Navy?'

'Yes, it's a cruel world, lad,' he said, 'and folk don't always get what they deserve.' He looked at the list. 'Get me two sets of signalling flags and a box of candles.'

2

Monkey business

The next hour flew by. Harry's arms and legs
ached. He never stopped running and
carrying. He was glad when Shadrach sent
him on an errand to the gunsmith's.

He loved going to Jeremiah Mumford's. He
would get to see George. George was his best
friend, even though he was twenty years old.
He had been teaching Harry to read and write
and work with numbers.

'Ask Mr Mumford if I can have some wads
for the large cannons,' Shadrach said. 'And
don't stand gawping at that ship while you're
out. Be quick.'

Harry ran along the quay, dodging between the people who were still coming and going. On his left, he passed the swordsmith's, the tailor's and the printer's. But there on his right, was the dock. And in the dock was His Majesty's ship, *Prosperity*.

It towered over everything and everybody. Harry had to put his head right back so he could see the top of the great masts. Each time he looked, it took his breath away. He could see the mighty cannons, poking from the gunports along the side of the ship.

He closed his eyes and imagined that he was part of the brave crew, going off to fight for their country with the famous Lord Nelson, Admiral of the Fleet.

He watched the sailors climbing the rigging. He admired the groups of officers, standing about talking in their smart uniforms.

He would go on a ship like that. Why should he worry about getting flogged? He would be the best sailor they ever had.

He hurried to the gunsmith's. As always, he looked up at the fine painted sign above the door: *Jeremiah Mumford, Supplier of Ball and Shot to His Majesty's Navy.*

'Well, hello there, young Harry,' said Mr Mumford. 'Shadrach will be busy today, I'll bet.'

Harry smiled and greeted Mr Mumford. 'Mr Pinchbeck said can he have some wads for the large cannons, please.'

'Aye, I expect they'll be for the *Prosperity*, are they? They say she sets sail tonight.'

'Yes, sir,' Harry said.

Mr Mumford went into the back room, and soon afterwards, George came out.

'Hello, Harry. Have you got time to do a bit of writing practice? I've left the top line of today's accounts free, so that you can write the date in if you like.'

They went into the office. Harry looked around. George laughed.

'Don't worry,' he said, 'it's still here.'

He pointed to the tall bookshelves.

There, perched on the top shelf, was a small brown monkey. It was watching Harry. Its bright little eyes blinked as George lifted a lantern so that Harry could see better. The monkey started to chatter softly.

'Can I feed it?' Harry asked.

'When you've done your writing practice,' George said. 'I've got some fruit you can give it.'

George placed a huge book on the desk and pointed to the top of a page. Harry often wrote in the ledger, and he was getting very good. George had said that soon no one would be able to tell the difference between Harry's writing and his own.

Harry picked up the pen and dipped it into the ink. He licked his lips as he worked. Carefully, he shaped each letter: *4th of October, 1805.*

When he'd finished, George nodded his head. It was a fine piece of writing. 'Well, I suppose I'd better get that fruit,' he said.

Harry looked around for the monkey. It had come down to a lower shelf.

Mr Mumford came in.

'That monkey's a right little nuisance,' he said. 'Don't know what to do with him now that my good lady's tired of him. Might have to do away with the little fellow.' Harry's eyes widened.

Mr Mumford looked at Harry's writing in the ledger.

'Well done, lad. There'll be a job here for you one day, if you want it. That is, if your head's not still full of going to sea.'

George returned with an apple. He took out his pocket knife and cut it into small slices. The monkey chattered excitedly.

'I've seen too many people go off in a ship and never come back,' Mr Mumford went on.

'But sir,' Harry said, politely, 'I'd rather fire guns than make them.'

George shook his head.

Mr Mumford laughed.

'I remember feeling the same way myself, Harry, when I was your age – till I understood how terrible war can be. You'll grow out of it.'

Harry silently promised himself he would not.

As George and Mr Mumford talked about the price of gunpowder, Harry took the pieces of apple from George and went over to the shelves.

The little monkey hopped up and down. It reached out and tried to snatch some slices from Harry's hands. Harry closed his hand tightly. The monkey screamed at him. Slowly, Harry opened his fingers. This time, the monkey, very gently, took a piece and popped it into his mouth.

'Have you thought of a name for him yet, sir?' Harry asked.

'No. He seems quite happy to be just "monkey",' the gunsmith said.

'Would you let me give him a name please, sir?' Harry asked.

'Can't see why not. Tell you what, next time I see you, tell me what his name is to be.'

Harry smiled and thanked him.

Mr Mumford pointed to a framed sampler on the wall. 'See that, lad? Mrs Mumford sewed that for me. Can you read it?'

'There's no place like home, sir,' Harry read out.

'That's right. You remember those words. The Navy's not for anyone who wants to live long and be happy.'

'What shall I tell Mr Shadrach, sir, about the wads?' Harry said, eager to change the subject.

'Tell him I'll send them over to him in half an hour.'

Harry thanked Mr Mumford, and waved to George. He took one last look at the monkey, and said goodbye.

George called after him. 'I'll not be giving you a lesson tonight, Harry. I'm going to the tavern for a drink with some mates.'

'Now don't do that, young George,' said Mr Mumford. 'Only fools will be out and about tonight. Home is the best place to be on the night that one of His Majesty's ships sets sail.'

'Why is that, Mr Mumford?' Harry asked.

'Never you mind, boy, and I hope you never find out. Now go on back to your master.'

3
A warning

Shadrach was looking at the huge piles of stores waiting to be taken to the *Prosperity*.

'Well, that's a good job done, Harry. We've earned our money today. I'll get you your tuppence and then you can go.'

Harry sat on a barrel to wait.

A loud voice from behind made him jump so much that he tumbled on to the dusty floor. 'Well, boy, don't just sit there. Get your master. Tell him Mr Swan is here to see him.'

It was the bosun.

'Yes, sir,' Harry said, and he ran off to get Shadrach.

As the two men talked, Harry watched and listened from the store-room door.

Mr Swan, the bosun, called outside to some men. They came in and began to heave the barrels and boxes on to their strong shoulders.

Mr Swan strode over to Harry and took him roughly by the arm.

'You as well, lad. Give us a hand. It might give you some manly muscles. You're like a bundle of bones.'

He gripped Harry's arm so tightly that Harry felt like crying out, but he kept his mouth shut.

'Er, Bosun, the lad's still needed here. He hasn't finished his work,' Shadrach lied.

'Now then, Chandler, am I to tell my captain you're not being helpful?' He smiled, showing his rotting teeth. 'If I say the lad helps, then that's the way it is,' he said, angrily. He pushed past Shadrach.

'All right, Mr Swan,' Shadrach said, 'but I can't spare him for long.' He looked at Harry. 'Better do as he says, son.'

'Bring those boxes,' the bosun snapped. He walked out of the shop.

Shadrach pulled Harry to one side, and whispered to him.

'Now listen, Harry, just go as far as the gangplank. No matter what happens, do not go on the ship. Do you hear me? Don't go on the ship.'

Harry understood the look on his face. 'All right, sir,' he said, 'I won't.'

Shadrach lifted the boxes and put them into Harry's outstretched arms.

4

On board

The boxes were heavy, but Harry was determined to keep up with the line of sailors. Everyone on the quay made way for them.

'Give those Frenchies a good thrashing, lads,' the pie-stallkeeper called as they passed.

'Don't you worry,' one of the sailors called back. 'Our big cannons will demolish Nappy's Navy. This war with the French has been going on too long.'

Harry knew that Nappy's Navy meant Napoleon's Navy.

Napoleon was the leader of the French: trying to conquer the whole of Europe. Lord Nelson was the leader of the English: trying to defend the country against a French invasion. George had told him that.

When the loading party reached the gangplank, they had to wait. Some sailors were leading some sheep aboard. Others were carrying crates of squawking chickens.

'Are they to be cooked for your meals?' Harry asked the seaman next to him.

The man laughed aloud. 'No, son,' he said, 'that meat would be too good for the likes of us. It's salt beef and maggot-ridden biscuits for us.'

'Maggots?' Harry said.

A sailor pushed him roughly in the back. 'Out of the way, monkey,' he said.

'Don't call me a monkey,' Harry called back.

The first seaman laughed. 'He thinks you're a powder monkey,' he explained to Harry.

'What's a powder monkey?' Harry said.

'It's a …'

But the rest of his words were lost in the shouts of the sailors, as they moved on to the gangplank.

Harry stopped. He desperately wanted to go on to the ship, but he knew he should do as Shadrach had told him. He put down the boxes and turned to go.

Suddenly, he was grabbed by the collar of his shirt. He felt it rip across his shoulder.

'Where do you think you're going, you idle little brat?' It was the bosun.

'I've got to go back to the chandler's,' he said.

'Pick up those boxes and take them on board, before I tan your hide.'

Harry decided to do as he was told. He struggled up the gangplank, trying not to trip.

It was hard to see where he was going, with the boxes he was carrying. Sailors pushed roughly past him.

Finally, he stepped off the gangplank and on to the deck of the ship.

He felt thrilled. He was actually on board the great fighting ship, *Prosperity*. If the bosun hadn't been so close by, Harry could have enjoyed the moment and had a good look around.

'See that?' the bosun growled at him, pointing to a ladder going down from the deck.

'Take the boxes down, then get back up here for some more.'

Harry had seen the other sailors go down this ladder. They had balanced the boxes and bundles on their shoulders. It looked easy enough, but the ladder seemed very narrow.

Carefully, he heaved two boxes on to his shoulder and turned to go down the ladder. It was really difficult, because he could only hold on with one arm.

As he disappeared below the level of the lower deck, he heard the bosun walk off.

Shaking with the effort and excitement, he reached the bottom. He looked around the gloomy areas of below decks. There was a horrible stale smell which caught his breath.

This must be the hold, he thought. It was a bit like the store-room at the chandler's, piled high with boxes, sacks and barrels.

He started to put his boxes on a barrel.

But before he could place them safely, he heard a voice.

'Look out below.'

He jumped out of the way as some sacks were lowered by rope.

'You two get down there and stack those sacks properly. And get the barrels lashed together,' yelled the bosun. 'I'll be down in a minute.'

'Aye, aye, sir,' came the reply, and two sailors came down into the hold.

Harry didn't want to catch the bosun's eye again, so he decided to hide behind the barrels. The boxes wobbled a bit as he crouched down.

He was just in time. The two sailors untied the sacks and stacked them in front of the barrels. He heard the bosun come heavily down the ladder.

'Now then, you two, I've got a special job for you tonight. You'll need a couple of mates to help you.'

The sailors made no reply.

'There'll be extra rations for you and money in your pocket if you do the job right,' he went on.

'Is it the usual job?' one asked, spitting on the floor.

'Aye,' the bosun said, 'the captain needs at least twenty more crew. And our little group has got to get half of them. So I want you to come with me to the taverns and we'll talk some likely lads into joining up.' He gave a cruel laugh. 'Know what I mean, lads? And if they're not too keen, just show them this, and don't take "no" for an answer.' He laughed again.

Harry peeped out to see what the bosun was holding up. It was a wooden club.

The bosun pushed it under the chin of one of the sailors, and jabbed it into his neck. The sailor staggered back, into the sacks, then fell backwards against the barrels.

'Meet me on the quay in half an hour,' the bosun growled, and he climbed up to the main deck.

The barrels tipped backwards, and the
boxes which Harry had hurriedly put on top
of them slid off. One of them crashed down
on to his head. He felt a sharp pain, and his
stomach heaved. Then the room around him
faded into blackness.

5

An unexpected journey

Harry woke in a panic. His mouth was dry, and he thought he was suffocating. It was dark except for a faint light coming from somewhere above him.

Something soft brushed against his face. Then something ran across his chest. He cried out. He brushed at his shirt and sharp teeth bit into his hand. He screamed.

As he tried to get up, the floor dipped sharply to his left and he rolled over. He crashed into something heavy.

Trying to get his breath, he lay as still as he could. Slowly, the floor dipped the other way and Harry tried to stop himself rolling once more.

Through the gloom, he saw boxes, sacks, barrels and huge coils of ropes. Then he spotted the dozen or more creatures gathered around him. Rats!

He kicked out wildly and waved his arms. They scurried away behind the barrels. Fear made him breathless. He tried to calm himself. He wished the floor would stop moving. Something was terribly wrong.

It was only when he became aware of the regular creaking sounds of the wooden ship, that he realized the awful truth.

Not only was he still aboard the *Prosperity*; it had set sail. He was at sea.

He touched his sore head and he tried hard to remember what had happened. Slowly, everything came back to him. He thought of his ma and Shadrach wondering where he was. The thought almost brought tears to his eyes. What was he going to do?

He looked up towards the light. He knew he would have to climb up there and find someone to help him. He hoped it wouldn't be the bosun.

Climbing the ladder was difficult because of the roll of the ship. At the top, he peered on to the deck. The air didn't seem any better than down in the hold. The place was gloomy, lit by only two or three lanterns.

Here and there, he saw men sitting and talking. Some were cleaning long lengths of heavy cable, others were playing a game.

They threw dice from a cup made of coiled rope, and they shouted at each other. Not far from the ladder, Harry saw some men in hammocks which were slung between the beams.

Taking a deep breath, he clambered from the ladder on to the deck. The ship heaved to one side and he stumbled, falling against one of the hammocks.

'Now then, me lad,' a voice called out, 'take it easy, now.'

'Sorry,' Harry mumbled.

The sailor looked at Harry's worried face and laughed. 'The first trip's always the worst, son. You'll soon get used to it.'

'But I'm not supposed to be here,' Harry said.

The sailor just laughed. 'Get in your hammock and rest while you can. You've a chance to be on rat-catching duty in a couple of hours.'

'I haven't got a hammock,' Harry said, staggering about as the ship dipped again.

'Well you can't sleep on the deck. You'll spend the night rolling about like a ball. You could lash yourself to one of the beams, if you like,' the seaman said.

'Over here, son,' another voice called out.

'You can have old Jem's hammock. He'll not be needing it, poor old soul. May he rest in peace.'

Harry muttered a thank you and scrambled towards the roll of canvas on the floor. A dead man's hammock was better than none.

The sailor showed Harry how to sling the canvas hammock between two beams.

Getting into it was the hardest part. The first three times he tried, he landed on the deck with a thud. On the fourth attempt, he managed to get in but immediately fell out the other side. He found himself laughing, in spite of everything.

'We'll make a sailor of you yet,' the seaman said, smiling. 'I'm Jack. Stick with me and you'll be all right,' he added.

Harry thanked him and wriggled around in his new bed. The sides of the hammock seemed to fold round him, squeezing his arms to his side, but it was much better than rolling about the deck. A few minutes later, he was fast asleep.

6

Fear and excitement

Jack tipped Harry out of his hammock. Men were calling to each other and taking down their hammocks.

'Come on, lad, up on deck. You don't want the bosun to catch you down below after the shout.' He pushed Harry up the ladder in front of him.

On the lower deck, there was a crowd of men. Harry stood behind Jack.

As he looked around him, he noticed other young boys. One of them looked really young. He had dark, curly hair and eyes that darted everywhere. When he saw Harry, he winked and gave him a cheeky grin. Harry found himself grinning back.

The bosun, Mr Swan, was yelling orders. Men and boys raced off to carry out their tasks.

The bosun moved towards the last group. 'Up to the top deck, you lot, and get those animals slopped out.'

The boy with the cheeky grin leapt ahead of the men and climbed the ladder easily.

Harry tried desperately to keep himself hidden. He froze as he heard the bosun call out to Jack.

'You and the lad, get back down to the orlop deck and lend a hand to the surgeon.' He laughed cruelly. 'He's got quite a few split skulls to attend to this morning.'

'Aye, aye, sir,' Jack said, and he dragged Harry back to the ladder.

He hasn't recognized me, Harry thought, overcome with relief. Perhaps things would be all right. This is what I wanted, isn't it? I'm on board one of His Majesty's ships, going to war against the French. I'm in the Navy!

A tap from Jack's foot brought him back to reality. 'Get a move on, lad.'

On the gloomy, stale-smelling orlop deck, about a dozen men were crouched on the floor. Some were holding their heads and groaning. Others just sat slumped forward, like half empty sacks of grain. Harry noticed blood on their faces and heads.

Behind them hung a dirty canvas acting as a curtain. From behind it came more groans.

'Who are they?' Harry asked Jack.

'Poor victims of the press gangs, lad,' he said. 'That's how the captain gets some of his crew. Men like the bosun hit them over the head, then carry them on board. When they wake up, they're in the King's Navy.'

Suddenly, Harry felt sick. A mixture of fear and excitement churned inside him.

The heavy atmosphere of the orlop deck
was threatening to suffocate him. Foul smells
filled his nostrils.

He wanted to be sick but his stomach was
empty. He just made awful retching sounds
which heaved at his stomach muscles. Jack
touched his shoulder.

'Hey, lad, take it easy. We're here to help the doc, not to get treated ourselves.'

But Harry felt his strength ebb away. He sat down and Jack crouched beside him.

'What you need, lad, is something to eat. Didn't you have a good feed before you came aboard? Most young 'uns do.'

Harry looked at Jack, struggling to be brave. He didn't deserve to be on board a great ship like the *Prosperity*.

Jack pulled Harry to his feet and took him away from the waiting men.

'What's up, lad? You'd better tell me. I can't be playing nursemaid.'

Harry bit his lip, and began telling Jack his story. When he'd finished, Jack ruffled his hair.

'No wonder you're feeling sorry for yourself. You should be back home with your ma.'

'But I really do want to be here,' Harry said. 'It's just a bit sudden, that's all.'

Jack laughed.

'Well then, welcome aboard, young sir. And let's get on with our job, before the bosun catches us. And speaking of the bosun, keep out of his sight as long as you can.'

For the next hour, Harry and Jack carried buckets of bloody water from behind the curtain up to the lower deck.

Once up there, they emptied the buckets overboard out of the gunports, where the great cannons stuck out of the sides of the ship.

The men were practising loading and firing them. Whenever Harry passed the men, they swore at him.

Back on the orlop deck, he helped Jack fill the buckets with fresh water from huge barrels.

He took them through the curtain, and as he did so, he stole a look at the seaman being treated by the doctor. He had his back to Harry.

The doctor appeared to be stitching up a gash on the young man's head. The man never made a sound.

'What are you gawping at?' the doctor
growled at Harry.

Harry decided not to reply. He just scurried
away through the curtain.

A few seconds later, the injured man came
out. Harry looked at his pale face. He felt a
shock go through him. The young man
looked straight at him.

'Harry!' he exclaimed. 'What on earth are
you doing here?'

Harry smiled. 'George!'

45

7

Rat hunt

The man and the boy hugged each other.
Jack looked puzzled.

'Come over here where we won't be
overheard. Tell me what's going on,' he
whispered.

Harry introduced George to Jack. While
Jack watched for the bosun, Harry told
George everything that had happened.

Then George told them his tale. He had
gone to the tavern for a drink with his mates.
When he left the tavern, he had been set
upon. He couldn't remember anything else.
He had woken up aboard *Prosperity*.

'The press gangs,' said Jack. 'Didn't anyone warn you about being out and about the night a ship sets sail?'

Harry and George looked at each other, remembering Mr Mumford's warning.

'What do we do now?' George said, his face even paler than before.

'There's nothing you can do, just grin and bear it. You're in the Navy now, so you'd better make the best of it.'

George gripped Harry's shoulder. 'At least we're in it together. We'll help each other through.'

'I reckon you need someone to keep an eye on both of you,' Jack said.

He lifted one of George's hands. It was pale and smooth with clean fingernails. He compared it to his own dark-skinned, leathery hand with its dirty, ragged nails. 'You've got the hands of a gentleman,' he said.

'I work in a gunsmith's. I write up all the accounts,' George explained.

Jack snorted. 'What am I taking on? A gentleman and a ...'

Harry thought he was about to say, '*baby*', but Jack stopped and looked at him and smiled. 'And a future captain of the King's Navy,' he said, slapping him on the back; 'with a bit of training from me, of course,' he added.

The three of them laughed and shook hands.

A loud voice called down to them. It was the bosun. He clattered down the ladder.

'Look lively there,' he called. 'Jack, you join gun-crew number three. You new lads get down in the hold and kill some rats. I want twenty dead 'uns by the end of the watch. Or there'll be trouble.'

He went back up the ladder.

'Come on, now, we've been chatting too long,' Jack said.

Minutes later, Harry and George stood in the hold looking at each other. They held the stout bits of wood Jack had given them.

'Have you ever killed a rat?' Harry asked. 'I usually just scare them away.'

'Yes, I have, but I can't say that I want to make a habit of it,' George said, twisting his face. 'How about if you drive them out and I'll do the rest,' he suggested.

Harry nodded.

About an hour later, Jack came down the ladder. They heard the sound of a bell above them.

'It's the end of the watch. How many have you got?' Jack asked George.

George pointed to the dead rats on the floor. 'Nineteen,' he said shrugging his shoulders.

'Let's hope he doesn't count them,' Jack said, looking worried.

He rummaged in his pockets and brought out a few biscuits. He offered them to Harry and George. They looked at the rats.

'I think we've lost our appetites,' George said.

'You'll feel better when you're back on the orlop. Come on.'

Jack helped George put the rats into a sack and they climbed the ladder once more.

The men were sitting at wooden tables or on the floor. Two of the sailors were giving out bowls and biscuits and pouring a strong-smelling liquid into tankards.

Jack found places for them at a table. He threw the sack of rats into a corner.

Harry noticed that the table was a broad plank, hanging from ropes attached to the wooden spars above. No matter how much the ship rolled about, the table hung there as level as could be. The bowls and tankards stayed in place.

'No grog for the lad,' Jack said to the sailor pouring the drinks, and he covered Harry's tankard with his hand. 'Plain water for you, me lad; don't want you getting drunk.'

Harry was disappointed. He wanted what the men had. Instead he got a drink of water which tasted stale.

He was surprised to find that he was hungry, and he crunched the hard cornmeal biscuit and looked for another. He munched happily as he listened to the men telling fascinating stories. He was just about to reach for another biscuit when he felt someone's eyes on him. The bosun was staring straight at him.

'Well, well, well,' he said, 'if it isn't the little bag of bones. How come you're still here?'

He reached out and pulled Harry to his feet. George began to rise from his seat, but Jack stopped him.

Harry swallowed his mouthful of biscuit, almost choking himself.

'And you, you pale-faced weakling,' the bosun added, jabbing his hand into George's chest, 'I've got something for you.'

He picked up a sack from the floor and emptied it on to the table. The dead rats went everywhere. They sent the bowls of food and biscuits flying.

Harry's stomach turned over as he looked at the sickening mixture of food and dead rats.

'Count them!' the bosun yelled at Harry.

His hands shook as he carefully counted the rats, pointing at each in turn.

The bosun's eyes narrowed as Harry reached the end of his count.

'Nineteen, sir,' he said, his voice coming out in a whisper.

'I've a good mind to flog you both!' he screamed at them. 'I wanted twenty!'

'Just a minute, Bosun,' said Jack. 'I found a dead rat over in the corner near the sack. It must have fallen out. I'll get it for you.' Without another word, Jack went off and brought back another rat. George and Harry watched in amazement as he flung it on the table with the others.

The bosun glared at the three of them. 'Get this mess cleared up,' he said.

Then he pulled Harry to one side and pushed his face close up to him. 'Now you're in the King's Navy, I've got just the job for you,' he growled. 'I will train you myself. We start in four hours.'

'What am I to be, sir?' Harry asked.

The bosun laughed. 'You, my lad, are going to be a powder monkey. What do you think of that?'

8

Powder monkey

Jack told Harry all about powder monkeys. They were young boys who brought the cartridges of gunpowder to the cannons.

The cartridges were kept in a part of the hold called the magazine. The boys had to fill a leather carrying case with cartridges and then shin up the ladders to the gun decks. The cartridges were then stored in a salt box, until the gun-crews loaded them into the cannons.

The boys had to be really speedy and be able to climb like monkeys.

Harry felt excited. It was such an important job.

He couldn't understand why George and Jack were looking so worried. He couldn't think of anything he'd rather be.

Even as the bosun dragged him to the middle deck, he didn't feel as frightened as before.

'Watch this gun-crew practising,' the bosun ordered. They stood near a huge cannon, which the bosun told him was a twenty-four pounder.

'Watch everything they do and the order they do it in. Learn it by heart, and keep a special eye on that monkey there. You'll replace him tomorrow.'

Harry looked at the young boy. The boy had come hurtling on to the deck and immediately emptied his bag of cartridges, stowing them safely in the salt box. Then off he went, disappearing below deck as quickly as if he had been thrown down below.

For over an hour, Harry watched the team of eight men. Each man had his own job to do. They loaded, aimed and pretended to fire the heavy black cannons.

The gun-captain told him that when they really fired the gun, the recoil was so great that it forced the cannon back a long way. Then the team would have to run the gun out again after each shot.

All this time, the young powder monkey flew up and down the ladders bringing the cartridges. Now and again, he would give Harry a tired smile.

When the bosun returned, Harry was fairly sure he knew the whole of the gun drill.

'The master says we can do it for real now,' the bosun told the gun-captain.

'Stand well back,' he told Harry, 'and watch the experts at work. We can fire three shots to the Frenchies' one.'

The next few minutes were the most exciting of Harry's life. He watched as the sponge on the long stick was thrust into the barrel of the cannon. This was to put out any sparks still there from shots fired earlier.

Then a new cartridge was passed along and put into the cannon. A member of the team, who was called the rammer, rammed it right into the barrel. Then a wad, just like those Mr Mumford sold, was put in. Then a huge cannon ball was placed inside and another wad after that.

Everything was ready for the fuse to be set and gunpowder poured into the top of the cannon.

Then some men aimed the cannon. They did this by wedging its barrel up or down, and heaving the gun-carriage to the left or right with long handspikes.

All this was done in less than a minute.

The gun-captain yelled, 'Stand clear.'

All of the gun-crew leapt to the sides and cowered down. One of them grabbed Harry and pushed him down beside them. Seconds later, there was a shout.

'Fire!'

There was the biggest bang Harry had ever heard. The air around him seemed to quiver, and he coughed as he breathed in smoke.

There was a loud rumbling sound as the huge cannon recoiled. It moved backwards about five yards!

Seconds later, the whole process began again. Harry's ears were ringing.

Before the next shot was fired, the bosun dragged him to the ladder. They went down to the orlop, then on down to the far end of the hold.

'This is the magazine,' the bosun said. 'Stay down here awhile and watch the monkey work.'

He started to climb up the ladder but leapt out of the way as the powder monkey came scurrying down. Only when the boy was safely down, did the bosun go up.

'He got out of the way for you,' Harry gasped in amazement. 'I thought he would trample on anyone who got in his way.'

The young boy laughed.

'It's a ship's rule,' he said, breathlessly. 'Get in the way of a powder monkey and you can be flogged.'

Harry smiled to himself. He hoped the bosun would get in his way as soon as possible.

9

Maggots taste cold

Days passed in a whirl of new experiences. Harry felt as though he worked, ate and slept in a strange world.

His time was spent working with the gun-crews. He worked so long and hard that even in his hammock, his legs felt as though they were still going up and down the deck ladders.

His head spun with new information. He learned about the different kinds of shot that went into the cannons. He learned how the ship relied on the sails and the winds to give it direction and speed.

He rarely saw George, except when they had meals. One of the petty officers had discovered that George could read and write and since then, George had been put to work by the ship's captain. Harry felt very proud of his friend and was glad that he had been given a gentleman's job.

George was also popular with the seamen; he would read newsletters to them and write letters for them.

At least Harry saw Jack all of the time. He was on the gun-crew that Harry monkeyed for. He was the sponger-out of the cannon.

They never had time to speak to each other, but it made Harry feel good to know he was there.

What disappointed Harry the most was that he rarely had time to spend on the upper deck. He wanted to look at the sea and feel the salty air on his face. He caught glimpses of the sky through the gunports. But it wasn't enough.

It was not how he'd imagined it would be.

And where were all of the other boys? He didn't go looking for them at meal-times, because he wanted to spend time with George and Jack. While on watch, they were too busy.

Powder monkeys flew around ignoring everything but their precious bag of cartridges. He did this himself. He had met the captain's shoe-boy a few times, and the five boys who worked in the galley, but they never really had time to talk.

It was the times he could spend with Billy
that were really special to him. Billy was the
young boy with the cheeky grin. He worked
up on the top deck. He looked after the
animals. He and Harry had become good
friends.

Billy was only ten years old. He had
stowed away after his parents had died, and
he had been with the *Prosperity* for almost
a year.

He had names for each of the pigs, sheep and chickens that he was looking after. He hated it when the men came and took them away for the pot.

The last time Harry had climbed up to see Billy, the marines in their bright red uniforms had chased him below again.

'Clear off, you dirty powder monkey,' one called.

Harry had scrambled back down to the lower decks. They had called him 'dirty'. He looked down at his ragged dirt-smeared clothes, and his bruised and grubby arms. He realized what a pathetic bundle of dirt and rags he had become.

He was beginning to feel sorry for himself. No, that won't help, he thought. I've just got to get on with it. But I really miss Ma, and home.

That night he whispered to George as they lay in their hammocks.

'When will we go home?' But George only snored. Harry didn't believe George was asleep: he just didn't have an answer.

When he rolled out of his hammock a few hours later, Harry felt better. Even if he was homesick, hungry all the time, and worn out from running up and down ladders, one thing was sure. He was going to be the finest powder monkey the *Prosperity* had ever had.

He stowed away his hammock and munched on a biscuit, ignoring the soft parts which he knew were maggots. If Jack and the rest could eat them, then so could he. When he got home, he would tell his ma something she didn't know: maggots tasted cold. That would make her laugh. Maybe she'd serve them up for supper.

At the end of the next watch, Harry was pleased to see George on the orlop. He was sitting with a group of seamen, reading from a newsletter.

'So what does it mean?' one asked.

'It means that we're going to join Lord Nelson's flagship, *Victory*. We're going to stop the French, once and for all.'

'Fighting alongside Lord Nelson,' Jack murmured.

'Yes, my friends,' George said. 'In a few days we will be in a great battle. We're going to war. We're going to save our country.'

Harry felt his heart beat faster. He was tired of all the practising. He was ready for the real thing.

Some of the men cheered. But some who had been in battles before stayed silent. Afterwards – long afterwards – Harry realized why. They knew that many good men would die, and they wouldn't all be Frenchies.

10

Action stations

Harry woke with a smile on his face. He had been dreaming of the gunsmith's shop. He was feeding the little monkey, while George wrote in his ledger. Everything was as it should be. He had done a day's work at the chandler's and he would take his tuppence home to his ma.

The sound of soft voices brought him back to reality. It was George and Jack talking. He listened.

'You've got to promise me, George.'

'I don't know if I can do that,' George replied.

'I'm telling you more men have died at the hands of the surgeon than in battle. He cuts off your arms or legs simply because he doesn't know what else to do.'

Harry heard George give a deep sigh.

'What exactly do you want me to do?' George asked.

'If I get some really bad wounds in the battle, throw me overboard. I'd rather face Davy Jones' locker than that kind of treatment. Please, George.'

Harry tried to peep at the two men, without tipping himself from the hammock. He watched them shake hands. Surely George hadn't agreed.

He was suddenly frozen with fear at the thought of losing either of these two good friends. And what about himself? He had never really thought about death, only the glory of winning and being part of the King's Navy.

Harry noticed that many men were already out of their beds, even though the bell hadn't sounded to start the next watch.

There was a buzz of excited chatter. Men were stowing away their hammocks. They were stuffing them along the side of the ship as extra protection against gunshots. Porridge had been brought from the galley and put on the tables.

George appeared at the side of his hammock.

'Come on, lad, there's a lot to do today. The word is, we're waiting for a signal from Lord Nelson. We've already sighted the rest of the fleet.'

Harry grabbed a biscuit and scrambled up the ladders towards the top deck. As his watch hadn't really started, he would use the time to go and see Billy.

He dodged the marines and the officer on watch, and moved toward the animal pen. As usual, Billy was lying in the pen on a pile of straw. The pigs snuffled around him.

'Billy, wake up.'

'Harry, what are you doing here?'

'We've reached the rest of Lord Nelson's fleet. Let's have a look.'

Billy scrambled to his feet and followed Harry to the far end of the deck. The two boys climbed up and looked over the side.

The sun was just coming up in a pink and blue sky. About half a mile away, rising and falling on the dark blue water, was a group of the finest fighting ships Harry had ever seen.

The English colours were flying proudly from the mast of the flagship. It was *HMS Victory* herself – the ship of Admiral Lord Nelson.

The two boys were speechless. Soon they would be part of the fleet.

The sound of eight bells told them one watch was finished and the next beginning. Harry told Billy he would try to see him later, then he scuttled back to the orlop.

The bosun was talking to the men. George stood at his side. He held a sheet of paper in his hand. The men fell silent as George read the message.

'On this, the 21st day of October, in the year of 1805, the Admiral Lord Nelson orders his fleet to prepare for battle. Today there will be battle with the French and Spanish fleets. We will fight to the death. No prisoners will be taken. A drum roll will sound action stations.'

Seconds later, men were racing to all parts of the ship. Harry made his way to his gun-crew on the middle deck.

He learned from the gun-crew that they were off Cape Trafalgar, near the Spanish port of Cadiz. It meant little to him. It was not England. That was all he understood.

He helped the men spread the decks with wet sand, to help prevent the gun-crew slipping.

'And to soak up the blood,' said someone.

Then he started his journeys back and forth to the magazine, collecting cartridges and placing them in the salt box. When it was full, the gun-captain told him to stand easy. That meant take a break until the next order came.

Harry sat with the men, who were eerily quiet. He wondered how Billy would manage, up on the top deck without any protection.

Suddenly he could hear officers arguing. It seemed that Lord Nelson had decided upon a different way of attacking the enemy.

Normally, the English and any enemy fleet would sail alongside each other in parallel lines, firing their rows of cannons at each other.

But this time Nelson had said only half the fleet would do this. The other half would come at the enemy from right angles.

One officer, who had been in Nelson's fleet before, said that it sounded crazy. The gun-crew began muttering amongst themselves as they discussed the new plan of action.

'But that will mean we can't fire at them until we're really close, and then we'll only have the end of the ship as the target,' a sailor said.

'Yes,' said Jack, 'but the enemy won't be able to shoot at us either. We'll have some kind of chance with our shots. They won't have any.'

A few minutes later, a drum roll began. The hairs on Harry's neck stood on end. Then he heard the shout.

'Action stations!'

The battle was about to begin.

11

Fire!

Harry crouched behind the gun-crew, shaking with a mixture of fear and excitement. They were waiting for the order to fire.

Through the gunport, he could see one of the line of ships come about and start sailing at right angles towards the French fleet and their Spanish allies.

A runner tumbled along the deck calling a message to all crew – a message from the Admiral Lord Nelson.

'England expects every man to do his duty.'

The words echoed from man to man. Harry heard others take up the cry. 'England expects every man to do his duty!' The message found its way through the ship.

Harry felt so proud. England needed him and all the men of the fleet. He would do his very best for England and Lord Nelson.

Suddenly, the air filled with the roar of the cannons of both English and enemy ships as they fired on each other.

The gun-crew's first shot boomed out and the great cannon threw itself back in recoil.

At the same moment, a splintering sound came from above, as chain shot from the enemy wrapped itself round their rigging. Part of the mast came crashing to the deck. Harry saw it hit a crew member. He stood transfixed, wondering what to do.

'Move, powder monkey!' The gun-captain kicked at him savagely.

Harry remembered his duties and ran off to the magazine for more cartridges. The leather carrying case, heavy with cartridges, thudded against his hip. He gasped for breath. The roars of the men and the terrifying booms of the guns filled his head and made his teeth ache and his throat vibrate.

Each time he returned to the gun, there were more injured men, but if they could still stand, they stuck to their posts. As he moved from deck to deck, he tried not to look at the men who were crying out in pain, or worse still, lying silent.

The air was heavy with smoke which burned the back of his throat and made him cough. The harder his breathing became, the slower he moved. He took shallow breaths, trying not to inhale too much smoke.

He tore a strip from his shirt and wound it lightly round his mouth, in the way some of the gun-crews did.

He filled the salt box for the third time, and took a moment to watch the gun-crew running out the gun again. Jack passed close to him.

'All right, young 'un?' he gasped to Harry. 'You're doing great.'

Harry grinned. He would run his heart out for men like Jack. He would ignore the noise and the smoke and do his duty.

He set off down the ladders again. This time he moved faster and started repeating Nelson's message to himself, matching the rhythm of his running. 'England expects every man to do his duty.'

This kept him going, even as he climbed over a sailor who had fallen on the ladder.

'England expects …'

He was still chanting to himself as he climbed back to the middle deck.

Halfway to his salt box, he stopped in his tracks. Something was very wrong.

There was a gaping hole in the deck where the great black cannon had stood.

Black smoke filled the air. Large sparks floated around his head. He saw some of the gun-crew lying on what was left of the deck. Their injuries were awful. Harry could hardly bear to look at them but he knew he must see if any of them needed help. And where was Jack? He couldn't bear it if one of those men was Jack.

He crouched down, trembling.

A faint cry for help came to him through the din of the battle. He looked around him. The cry came again.

It was Jack. He was swinging in mid-air, hanging from a piece of the broken deck. The beam he was clinging to was bending and creaking dangerously. Far below him were the guns of the lower deck. If he fell, he would be smashed to pieces.

'What shall I do?' called Harry, getting as near to the edge as possible.

'Find a rope. Tie it to something strong. Pass the end to me and I'll haul myself up.'

Harry looked around frantically.

He found a coil of rope lying just behind his salt box. His hands shook as he pulled out a length. He ran to the side of the ship, tied it to a spar that looked intact, and unrolled the rest.

'Hurry, lad,' Jack called, 'I'm near to dropping.'

As Harry rushed back, there was a loud splintering sound and the wooden spar cracked and began to split.

Harry saw Jack lose the grip of one of his hands and swing wildly.

Quickly, he lowered the rope and Jack reached for it with his free hand. But the deck gave way completely, throwing Harry on to his back. He screamed as Jack vanished from sight. Harry crept to the gaping hole, praying that Jack was on the end of the swinging rope.

He was there; white-faced and gasping for breath, but he was safe.

He started to pull himself upwards. Harry bent forwards to help him but Jack sent him back, fearing they would both go down.

Jack finally scrambled on deck, just as the ship was hit again. There were screams from men at the other end of the deck, as bits of mast and sail crashed down around them. But still, those gun-crews who were able continued firing.

Jack and Harry clung together. 'Thanks, lad, you're a fine shipmate.'

Harry's eyes stung with emotion and smoke.

'Come on, we'd better see if we can help the other guns. Follow me.'

They picked their way between the piles of timber, canvas, and the dead and dying. Harry tugged at Jack's arm.

'Jack, I want to go and see if Billy's all right.'

'No, lad. I've heard the top deck has just about had it. Some of it's gone.'

'Well, what about George?' Harry went on.

'Listen,' Jack said, roughly, 'the battle's not over yet. You don't think of others till your duty's done.'

'Sorry,' Harry murmured.

For the next hour, Harry became powder monkey for gun-crew number four. Their own poor lad had been hit. But the team had been luckier than most, and they still had their gun-captain. Jack took over from the rammer who was badly injured.

The battle continued. They heard men saying that the ships which had sailed in the new formation had caused great damage to the French and Spanish ships. Some whispered that victory might be in their grasp.

As Harry returned out of breath from another run to the magazine, a rough-looking sailor was waiting for him.

'You the powder monkey who's got a friend called George? The one who reads and writes?'

Harry nodded.

'Well, he wants see you up on the next deck. He's been hit. He's been hit bad.'

12

Victory at a price

As soon as Harry found someone to replace him, he raced up to the next deck. He dodged between the dying and the injured until he found George. He was propped up in a sitting position, with one bloodied arm hanging helplessly at his side. His face was badly cut.

'George, I'm here. What happened?'

'Never mind that,' George said. He called to an officer.

'This is the lad I told you about. He can write the messages down for me.'

An officer shoved paper, pen and ink at Harry, and looked out of the port-hole towards the flagship. 'Just write down the signals as I call them out to you. Do you understand?' the officer said.

Harry nodded, nervously. He watched his friend's face grow grey with pain.

Minutes passed. There seemed to be less firing from both the *Prosperity* itself and the enemy.

Now and then, men would cheer and cry out as they watched French and Spanish ships burst into flames, or begin to sink.

Suddenly the officer began to read a signal to Harry. 'A – great – victory – is – in – sight. Our – gallant – Admiral – Lord – Nelson – lies – dying – from – a – sniper's – bullet.'

Harry and George looked at each other. A wonderful leader was dying. The Battle of Trafalgar was almost won, but the hero of the hour wouldn't live through it.

'Take it to the captain, Harry,' George said, weakly.

A minute later, he and another lad were sent off running round the ship, giving the news. There were no cheers at the thought of certain victory, only sadness at the news about Lord Nelson.

There had been no cannon fire for a few minutes.

Men had started to clear up the mess on the decks and do what they could for the injured.

Harry made his way to the top of the ship – he had to find Billy.

A sorry sight met his eyes. Some of the deck was gone. Parts of the little pen, where Billy had tended his animals, were scattered everywhere.

There was no sign of Billy.

Harry bit hard into his lip. He knew that Billy would have stayed with his animals, right to the last moment. But surely he couldn't be dead.

Harry called out as loudly as he could. 'Billy! Billy! Where are you?'

Harry went over to where the pigs lay and stood in silence as men moved around him.

Something stirred beneath the heavy weight of the pigs.

Harry moved closer. Suddenly, a hand appeared from behind one of the pigs' heads and reached out.

With a cry of joy, Harry grasped the hand and pulled. Within seconds, a small boy wriggled free.

'Billy!' Harry cried, hugging him, 'you're alive!'

Billy smiled. 'There was a blast and I got knocked off my feet. Then the pigs fell on me. The poor beasts got the worst of it. I suppose they saved me really.'

* * *

Back on the middle deck, the bosun was mustering the crew and giving orders. Soon the men would be able to stand down and get some food and rest.

It was good to be alive.

Several weeks later, as the sun came up, Harry and Billy sat on deck, counting the numbers of maggots in their biscuits. George was sitting near them with his arm bound up in a sling and a much better colour in his face.

Jack, who had come through with only a few scratches, slept in his hammock.

They had been to Gibraltar for repairs, but once again they were at sea.

The ship rolled gently. The wind swelled the new sails and whistled round the rigging.

They were going home.

There's no place like home

People lined the quay, as the *Prosperity* sailed into harbour. News of their victory and the death of Lord Nelson had reached England on the fifth day of November.

George and Harry strained their eyes to see if their families were there. Surely, after their disappearance, they would have guessed where they had gone. Such things had happened often enough before.

Even though Billy had no family of his own to look for, he too stretched over the rail, scanning the quay.

'It's Ma!' cried Harry. 'I'm sure I can see Ma.'

'And Shadrach, and Mr Mumford,' added George.

Minutes later, Harry tumbled into his mother's arms, not even attempting to hide his tears of joy. They hugged each other, over and over again.

'Oh, I've hoped and prayed you were on this ship today. I was so afraid you'd been killed,' she cried.

Harry dragged Billy forward to meet his ma.

She was charmed immediately by his cheeky grin.

'You must stay with us,' Harry heard her say.

Shadrach and Mr Mumford came over and shook Harry by the hand. Shadrach slapped him on the shoulder. 'Well, I suppose earning tuppence a day will be too tame for you now, eh?' he said.

'No, sir. I'll start again tomorrow if I can bring Billy too,' Harry said. The men laughed.

'You mean you're not signing up for another sea trip?' Mr Mumford said.

Harry blushed, but said nothing.

'Well, before you go off home,' the gunsmith went on, 'I've got something for you back at the shop.'

* * *

In the back room, Mr Mumford took the sampler down from the wall. He pointed to the beautifully embroidered words.

'There's no place like home,' he said. 'Let this remind you.'

He handed it to Harry. Harry thanked him.

He knew he didn't really need it. He had his own reminders; too many of them. His dreams would be filled with them.

They'd be very different to the dreams he'd had before going to sea and to war. And he never wanted to handle a gun again, unless it was to clean it.

'And another thing,' Mr Mumford said, 'do you remember what I said you could do the next time we met?'

Harry looked puzzled. Then it came to him. 'The little monkey!' he cried. 'You said I could name the monkey.'

'That's right, lad.'

Mr Mumford went into the other room and returned with the small creature. It chattered to itself as he handed it over to Harry.

Harry laughed as it began picking through his hair with its tiny fingers.

'Well, lad. He's all yours if you want him. So what's it to be? Give him a name.'

'I've got the perfect name for him,' Harry
said, smiling at everyone.

The little monkey looked at Harry with its
bright, beady eyes.

'I name him "Powder",' he said.

About the author

I'm headteacher of a
primary school, so most
of my writing has to be
done in the school
holidays. The story of
Harry, the powder
monkey, first came to
me while I was visiting

a museum. There was a life-
size reconstruction of an old fighting ship.
I stood and looked at it for ages.

In my mind I could see the many young
boys who were used on board those ships to do
hard and dangerous jobs. Over the next few
days, Harry's story came to me. After a great
deal of research, I wrote *The Powder Monkey*.

Other Treetops books at this level include:
The Worst Team in the World by Alan MacDonald
Paradise High by Annie Dalton
A Spell of Trouble by Alan MacDonald
Soccer Showdowns by Rob Childs
The Ghosts of Bracken Hill by Ann Mackintosh

Also available in packs
Stage 15 pack D   0 19 918730 4
Stage 15 class pack D   0 19 918731 2